William Howe Downes

I. M. Gaugengigl: His Life and Works (1883)

William Howe Downes

I. M. Gaugengigl: His Life and Works (1883)

ISBN/EAN: 9783742845986

Manufactured in Europe, USA, Canada, Australia, Japa

Cover: Foto ©Raphael Reischuk / pixelio.de

Manufactured and distributed by brebook publishing software
(www.brebook.com)

William Howe Downes

I. M. Gaugengigl: His Life and Works (1883)

John A. Lowell & Co.

Art Rooms,

No. 70 KILBY STREET, BOSTON, MASS.

PICTURES BY SOME ARTISTS WHOSE WORKS
ARE NOT SEEN IN ANY OTHER
GALLERY IN THE WORLD.

I. M. GAUGENGIGL,

CHARLES SPRAGUE PEARCE,
Medal of 1880

WILLIAM E. NORTON,

GEORGE W. EDWARDS,

and Others.

JOHN A. LOWELL & COMPANY,
BOSTON.

I. M. GAUGENGIGL:

HIS LIFE AND WORKS.

WITH DESCRIPTIONS AND CRITICISMS OF HIS
PRINCIPAL PAINTINGS.

EDITED BY

William Howe Downes

BOSTON:

PUBLISHED BY JOHN A. LOWELL & CO.,
MASON BUILDING, 70 KILBY ST.

1883.

NOTE.

A NEW PHASE of art patronage has been inaugurated by JOHN A. LOWELL & Co., of Boston, whose policy is different from that of any other establishment in the United States. The system adopted consists of an arrangement with certain leading American artists by which the firm takes all the pictures they produce, the artists on their part being bound to sell to no one else. Among the men of exceptional talent who have been introduced to the public and who have been enabled to secure a wider recognition by this means, Mr. GAUGENGIGL stands foremost.

It is the purpose of this *brochure* to make him still more widely known and appreciated; and in this connection it may be remarked that one reason why his pictures have not been more familiar to the general public, outside of Boston, is that they have been bought by Boston connoisseurs as soon as finished. The presence of one of his paintings in a collection, either public or private, has come to be regarded as necessary to the completeness of the collection: and there is no doubt that his work strengthens any collection to which it is added, because it is unique, and the best of its class. So far as the system of co-operation, to which reference has been made, has been pursued it has proved highly satisfactory to both parties. One result of it has been a decided advance in the prices of Mr. GAUGENGIGL's works. These delicate and masterly cabinet paintings have appreciated in value very rapidly, and now command prices three times as high as were formerly asked for them.

Apart from the share of credit due to JOHN A. LOWELL & Co. for this gratifying circumstance. the firm is entitled to the thanks and substantial support of every lover of art in the country for the services it has rendered to native art and artists in buying outright as it does, direct from the studios of the strongest Americans, both here and abroad, the works by which our artists are winning international renown and honors.

IGNAZ MARCEL GAUGENGIGL.

MR. GAUGENGIGL was born in Passau, Bavaria, in 1855. He graduated from the Gymnasium in Munich, and afterwards became a student in the Academy under Professor Raab. Then he painted in the studio of Professor William Diez. After leaving the Academy he studied portrait painting and received orders from the King of Bavaria, painting for his majesty, *The Hanging Gardens of Semiramis.* Later he went to Italy to continue his studies, and in 1878 visited the Paris Exhibition. From Paris he came to the United States, and has since that time pursued his profession in Boston, with a success as gratifying as it is remarkable. Mr. Gaugengigl's strong decorative instincts and unerring taste have caused a demand for his services in the way of interior decorations which he rather reluctantly yielded to. His only work of

importance in this field was that done in
the Boston Museum, where he painted the
much-admired panel above the stage, his
design consisting of a procession of rosy
cherubs bearing Spring flowers towards an
imaginary artist ; *Fame* might be considered
a far-fetched title for the work, but such is
the idea, and certainly nothing could be
more cheerful or winsome than the jolly
cherubs with their fragrant burdens. He
also furnished the design from which the
ceiling of the Museum auditorium was
painted — a blue sky flecked with fleecy
clouds. The success of these decorations
led to several orders for work in a similar
vein in private residences, but Mr. Gaugengigl much prefers the liberty of imagination
and the pleasing conceits permitting so much
more latitude in easel pictures. Usually he
goes to Germany during the summer vaca-
tion, to visit his parents, his father being a
professor of Oriental languages in the
Bavarian capital.

MR. GAUGENGIGL'S PAINTINGS.

MR. GAUGENGIGL has been called the "Meissonier of America," but, though this title may convey to one who has not become familiar with his works some idea of his style, and though it is true enough that there are certain external points of resemblance, it is doubtful if this compliment would be entirely acceptable to a man who has striven so hard for originality and whose productions have such a unique flavor. We like to compare a favorite painter's pictures with those of the great masters of the art, but comparisons of this nature are not less tempting than perilous; they are as liable to do injustice to the originality and quality of the performance we would praise as they are to overstep the bounds of truth and modesty. It is therefore as inexpedient to call Mr. Gaugengigl the "Meissonier o America," as it is to name Colorado the

"Switzerland of America," ● Boston the "Athens of America." In certain respects there are good reasons for preferring Colorado to Switzerland, and Boston to Athens. and in all respects it is certainly wiser and better to let our own scenery, social system, art and institutions stand on their own MERITS.

One of the critics has found features of similarity between Mr. Gaugengigl and Vibert, whose pictures are remarkable for delicacy of touch and nice feeling for color; there is much to justify this comparison. Nothing could be more clever than Mr. Gaugengigl's paintings, many of them not much larger than the palm of a man's hand. " The peculiarly modish and pleasing quality of Mr. Gaugengigl's works," says the *Boston Daily Advertiser,* "is a more subtle affair than is generally supposed. If they were not unique they would be far less attractive. Vibert alone possesses this delicate, humorous 'high-life' flavor in a higher degree, with the same or not much greater perfection of technique. Meissonier's more exalted motives place him in a different and superior rank, even if his skill did not put him beyond comparison. When he is trivial, comparatively speaking, he descends to the same level of *genre*, and in this vein he is no greater than Vibert, when the latter is at his best. Mr. Gaugengigl resembles Vibert, but he has never been so ambitious, perhaps because he feels his limitations." Speaking of the artist's painting of himself at work in his studio, the *Boston Journal* remarks : " It is based upon a very familiar subject, but his treatment of it is so original and fresh that it has all the force of a new departure. There is here a method which no other painter in this country, at least, employs, and which has in it the elements evident in the works of Meissonier and of those unrivaled old Dutch painters from whom even he has drawn much inspiration." The *Globe* (June 25,

1882) remarks with great justice of Mr. Gaugengigl: " He is complete master of all the changing shades of expression that flit across the human countenance, and he can arrest whatever one he desires and portray it to the life."

The *Boston Post* points out in the following paragraph the instructive lesson furnished by Mr. Gaugengigl's career to all artists who imagine that success can be achieved in any other way than by slow, devoted and painstaking work : " A steadfast adherence to these principles has been the characteristic of Gaugengigl's art life and the secret of his success. If, as has been said, great genius is only great patience, this artist is surely entitled to the rank of genius. The old Latin motto *festina lente*, deserves to be inscribed above his easel, and at any rate is evidently carried steadily in his mind from year to year. During the three years of his residence in this city he has painted only twenty-five pictures, and has reaped the reward of this conscientious, patient work by attaining to a height of financial and artistic success that he could never have secured had he been content to throw off fifty or more mediocre pictures a year, as not a few ordinary artists are willing to do. As one result of this method, each successive picture that he has painted has been superior to those which had preceded it, and his work shows a steady, upward growth and improvement." In a sketch of his life, printed 1882, the *Sunday Times* says "he interprets the very dignity of art, and in the gentleness of his spirit he combines with it a tender and refined feeling. In the selection of his subjects or incidents he is always happy, as well as in composition and arrangement of accessories."

Below we give a list of Mr. Gaugengigl's principal pictures, many of which are in the possession of private owners in Boston, New York and other cities. *The Student*, owned by Thomas Wigglesworth, Esq., of

Boston, was stolen from the gallery where it
was on exhibition, and has never yet been
recovered, though a reward of $100 was
offered for information concerning its whereabouts by John A. Lowell & Co.

THE MUSICIAN.
THE PHILOSOPHER,
READING,
THE STUDENT,
HOW DO YOU DO?
SMALL AUDIENCE,
THE TROUBADOUR.
MISCHIEF,
THE YEAR,
STIRRUP CUP.
GOING OUT,
THE PETS.
ONE OF THE COMMITTEE OF PUBLIC SAFETY,
SIESTA,
IDYLLE,
HIS HOBBY,
A STUDIO,
THE SURPRISE.
LE REFUGIÉ,
AN AFFAIR OF HONOR.

ADAGIO,
THE AMATEUR.
BELLISSIMA.
INCREDULITY,
QUIET AFTERNOON,
THE CHILD IS FATHER OF THE MAN.
AND DRIVE DULL CARE AWAY,
REVENGE,
EGALITÉ.

The press criticisms which follow have been collected for the purpose of showing the general estimate of Mr. Gaugengigl's works. Many of his pictures are graphically described, and we can only say that the newspaper critics, as a rule, while devoting columns of space to every new work by Mr. Gaugengigl, have in hardly a single instance found occasion to utter a word of censure.

OPINIONS OF THE PRESS.

The Daily Advertiser.
[In a notice of the Paint and Clay Club Exhibition.]
BOSTON, Dec. 11, 1881.

Concerning I. M. Gaugengigl's five pictures, it would be difficult to say enough in the way of praise without being or seeming extravagant. This is the greatest exhibit Mr. Gaugengigl has ever yet made at any exhibition. His new canvas, called " His Hobby," has been described : but no description could do justice to its unction, its delicate drollery, its grasp of character, or the Meissonier-like skilfulness and mastery shown in its execution.

The Sunday Courier.
BOSTON, Jan. 29, 1882.

This painting promises to be one of the most interesting and artistic that has been produced by Mr. Gaugengigl; let us look at it. The landscape, (very well treated and refreshingly airy and luminous) deals with a stretch of sea beach. Four figures are visible upon the sands. A most dramatic group it is. A duel has been

fought, and one of the combatants lies on his
back. his right hand extended, still grasping his
blade. The victor is standing a little apart. just
sheathing his sword, and striking a haughty attitude. One of the seconds bends over the
wounded, perhaps dying, man. All are dressed
in the old Spanish costumes, so called, brilliant
and gay in color. On the crest of a neighbor-
ing dune stands waiting the carriage — one of
those curious old vehicles hung on straps —
which is to bear away the belligerents and their
friends. The grouping and posing of the figures leaves nothing to be desired. The picture
tells its story powerfully. There is no other
artist in Boston who does this sort of thing,
though there must be some who would like to.
It is, perhaps, essentially a European province
of art. and you would hardly expect a North
American Yankee to turn out these exquisite
genre paintings.

Among the paintings he has produced since
he came to Boston are THE PHILOSOPHER,
HOW DO YOU DO? SMALL AUDIENCE, a
gentleman reading aloud with theatrical ges-
tures and great facial contortion to a solitary
and apparently unmoved auditor; THE PETS, a
lady feeding birds from her hand, owned by

Miss Faulkner of Arlington Street; SUMMER, a coquettish girl puttting on her gloves, an original etching of which appeared in the *American Art Review*; MISCHIEF, a laughing ideal head which Mr. Gaugengigl also etched for the *Review*; THE SURPRISE, a cavalier implanting an unctuous kiss upon the neck of a young woman in an eighteenth century toilette; AN IDYLL, a landscape with diminutive figures of a pair of lovers strolling on a hillside path; HIS HOBBY, an elderly gentleman scrutinizing with great seriousness and an air of profound knowledge a collection of paintings in a gallery; HIS STUDIO, the interior of his own room, with himself in it, seated before his easel. THE IDYLL and HIS HOBBY were shown at the late exhibition of the Paint and Clay Club, of which Mr. Gaugengigl is a member; MISCHIEF was in the Museum of Fine Arts last year; HIS STUDIO was in the recent exhibition of the Philadelphia Academy; and the others have been exhibited at various places.

The Journal.

[In notice of Art Club Exhibition.]

BOSTON, Feb. 18, 1882.

Turning to single figures which have more or

less of incident to give them a purpose, we shall very soon find pleasure in examining the work of Mr. Gaugengigl and Mr. Hovenden, which in refinement of technique have an element in common, although the inspirations and subjects are widely diverse. These two pictures are easily the best of their class in the collection, the former, representing the artist himself at work in his studio, showing a quiet, intellectual enjoyment in art for itself, and the latter describing an aged and laughing negro, indicating the combination of an unusual appreciation of character with a technical skill which is very nearly perfect.

* * * * * * *

This picture is undoubtedly the best that Mr. Gaugengigl has yet painted, and confirms the belief in the steady advance in his art which those who have observed his career most closely have been led to entertain. The quiet and unostentatious character of the effort is likely to deceive some who are prone to consider a picture weak unless it is sensational, but a little observation will show a wealth and harmony of color, a completeness of composition, a perfection of drawing, and an agreeable and natural

effect of light and atmosphere which is only to
be gained by complete knowledge and great
fidelity and skill. The figure, small as it is
when measured by inches, is large in its expression of life and action, keeps its place in
the middle distance admirably, and is evidently
earnestly engaged about something, not simply
sitting for its portrait, as so many personages
in similar works appear. It would be easy to
write much about this picture without exhaust-
ing the expressions of admiration which it calls
forth, but when all are reckoned up the sum
would be the opinion that it is a rare work, and
one which no other American painter of like
subjects is able to produce.

The Independent.

March 1st, 1882.

Let us close this first paper with a pleasant
word, and one may justly say a pleasant word of
that charming painter with the unpronounceable
name of Gaugengigl. The little picture which
he sends to the Art Club has been already
exhibited in Philadelphia, and it is worthy to go
the rounds of all the exhibitions in the country.
It is a studio interior, with a portrait of the

artist's self at his easel. The figure is so well drawn, the values so true, the composition so harmonious, the execution at once so free and so finished that it almost needed the awkward piece of sham armor in the corner as a foil to so much excellence.

The Press.

PROVIDENCE, March 7th, 1882.

Here may be seen also the exquisite Meissonier-like picture, Mr. Gaugengigl's last little gem. A fair young dame in the Directoire costume, which the artist so often and with such fine effect paints, walks daintily down a corridor. A lover — the haughty chevalier — has seized mademoiselle around her dainty waist, and is imprinting a kiss upon the rosy cheek, which act paralyzes poor little mademoiselle so that she cannot move, but stretches out her pretty arms imploringly and screams — aloud, of course — for her chaperone, who is probably not far off. The action, costuming and painting of these tiny figures is masterly.

The Folio.

BOSTON, May, 1882.

A consideration of this picture naturally leads

to a mention of I. M. Gaugengigl, a young
painter from Munich, who became enamored of
the American students gathered there, and
drifted hither with some of them, and has been
painting here for two or three years.   His
subjects are for the most part character studies
in interiors of Meissonier dimensions, almost
photographic in detail, yet never betraying
any other photographic idea, and possessed
of a feeling or a spirit, according to the subject, perfect in its way.   He has been taken up
lately by John A. Lowell, and his later pictures
are bringing prices unheard of heretofore for
such small canvases.   His last-finished work,
now at Mr. Lowell's, contains two figures, a
youth and a maid, the former mischievous and
the latter frightened.   A stolen kiss.   That is
all.   But the color is marvellous.   His costumes
are variously of the fourteenth, fifteenth or
sixteenth centuries, and the textures and colors
of the gowns worn by his maidens and matrons
would woo even the veriest Philistine to a
belief in the æsthetic.   A view of his studio,
with himself sitting at an easel, busily at work,
was shown here recently, and sold immediately,
with a chance a few days afterward, to get
double the price.

The Daily Advertiser.

BOSTON, May 6, 1882.

The latest work from the brush of I. M.
Gaugengigl, now on view at John A. Lowell &
Co.'s gallery, is entitled LE REFUGIÉ, and
possesses an unusual interest, owing to the
serious dramatic character of the subject. **Mr.**
Gaugengigl's immense skill has hitherto been
employed upon agreeable but entirely dilettante
compositions with a flavor of eighteenth-century
elegance which could make but a passing
impression because of their remoteness from
the actualities of today, and, although he has
not yet got his heroes out of their becoming
small clothes, it is pleasant to see that he has
in this instance introduced an element of sober
human interest quite removed from the ameni-
ties of the last-century drawing room. The
painting in question represents a young Huguenot gentleman who has narrowly escaped falling
a victim to the fury of a mob, and is depicted
just at the moment when he has knocked at the
door of a friend, and is anxiously awaiting a
response to his summons. The expression of
his comely face, as he leans forward in an
attitude of intense suspense, listening **for a**

footfall behind the door, is very forcibly rendered and full of significance. This, and the
pose of the figure, drawn with the utmost
ability and success, expresses his anxious state
of mind in a striking way, and tells the story
marvellously well. The execution of this little
masterpiece is beyond all praise, and is near
enough perfection to confirm the most enthusi-
astic predictions of those who have all along
perceived the artist's exceptional talent and
believed in his capacity to apply it to aims and
topics which should be worthy of it. It would
be impertinent to urge him to depart from a
class of subjects for which he has a special
predilection; but since he has in some degree
inaugurated a new departure himself, it is perhaps allowable to express the hope that he will
take up some characters of contemporaneous
interest and tell us a story of our own times.—
which, after all, and in spite of the matter of
clothes, are of the greatest moment to us who
have to live now.

The Courier.

Boston. May 7th, 1882.

Some years ago a picture painted by I. M.
Gaugengigl for Mr. Wigglesworth was stolen

from the gallery where it was on exhibition, and J. A. Lowell & Company now offer a reward of $100 for its recovery. It was called THE STUDENT, and represented a gentleman in white wig, white satin coat and breeches, white silk stockings, leaning over a side-board to examine a map of France, upon which he rests both hands. A chair upholstered in reddish stuff, a yellow curtain on right, a mandolin on wall, and blue vase in left-hand corner, make up the accessories. It is time this sort of thing were stopped, and editors interested in art will at once confer a favor and do a service to all artists by reprinting this note, since it may thus meet the eye of some one who has seen the picture.

The Courier.

BOSTON, May 7, 1882.

I. M. Gaugengigl's latest picture, LE REFU-GIÉ, is to be seen at Lowell's gallery, and must be welcomed by this clever artist's already large circle of admirers as marking an advance in his art, as every new work should do. It represents the fugitive knocking in suspense and solicitude at the door of a friend for shelter from his pursuers. The modelling and pose of the figure are firm and good, the expression of the countenance capital, and the color has the excellencies which distinguish all Mr. Gaugengigl's work.

The Herald.

BOSTON, May 7, 1882.

Gaugengigl has recently completed one of his unique little figure pictures, which may be seen at John A. Lowell & Co.'s gallery. It is called THE REFUGEE. The figure of a young Frenchman, in picturesque attire, of course, is presented at the door of a house, a part of the stone portico of which is seen. The young fellow is pressing against the door, and, with his head in a listening position, seems to be straining his sense of hearing to find out if he is to be speedily let in. His face wears a seriously intent expression and the figure is alert in sympathy with the face. The whole scene is capitally well portrayed. The scale of color in the rough stones of the street, brick portico, from which the paint, or stucco, is partly worn, dark door and the grave lines of the coat and hat of the youth is grayish and

cool, and therefore, the interest of the work
centres in the drawing and action of the figure
and the motive of the scene. Mr. Gaugengigl
has made an advance upon the presentation of
the merely pretty in this expressive picture.
Another picture by this artist, THE SURPRISE,
which was shown at the St. Botolph Club, is
also in this gallery now. In a gold frame,
instead of a bronze, as formerly, it looks like
quite another painting. It is a spirited, humorous fancy.

The Gazette.

BOSTON, May 7, 1882.

Mr. Gaugengigl has placed on exhibition at
the gallery of Messrs. J. A. Lowell & Co., one
of the strongest pictures we have seen from his
hand. It is called THE REFUGEE, and represents
a Huguenot, who has escaped from his pursuers,
knocking at a friendly door for shelter. The
facial expression is remarkably fine, and the
pose is eloquent in suspense. The whole work
is highly dramatic in the most refined sense of
the word. There is a force and vigor in this
charming canvas quite in keeping with the
subject, and wholly different in character from

anything the artist has previously exhibited
here. The drawing is, of course, perfect. The
color is beautiful in harmony, and the textures
are finished with the greatest care and with the
most charming effect. A more delightful or a
more masterly little gem of painting in its kind
it would be difficult to imagine.

The Times.

BOSTON, May 7, 1882.

Mr. I. M. Gaugengigl has completed his best
picture. It is entitled LE REFUGIE. The figure
of a man stands at an archway door listening
for a reply to a secret knock he has given.
Strong in modelling, refined in color and in-
tensly interesting in story, it makes his reputa-
tion as a figure painter of the highest order. It
is in the hands of Messrs. Lowell & Co.

The Traveller.

BOSTON, May 9, 1882.

Mr. John A. Lowell shows a new picture from
Gaugengigl,—THE REFUGEE — which is beyond
doubt the finest work this artist has yet
achieved. The subject represents a young

Huguenot who has just escaped the violence of
a mob, and who stands knocking at a friend's
door for admittance. The intentness of the
attitude, the expression of face and figure. is
wholly within the domain of artistic insight,
and it registers an advance on the part of Mr.
Gaugengigl, from a skillful and delicate mastery
of technique to the entrance of the spiritual
mysteries of art.

The Journal.

BOSTON, May 13, 1882.

Mr. I. M. Gaugengigl has a new picture on
exhibition at Mr. John A. Lowell's gallery, No.
70 Kilby street. It represents a young man.
who is clad in the costume of a Huguenot and
has evidently made his escape from some pur-
suer, standing and knocking at a stout door and
anxiously awaiting admittance. The picture,
like all of Mr. Gaugengigl's works, is beautifully painted. pure and clear in tone and very
skilful in drawing and color. It is also more
spirited in action than most of his works, and in
quite a new vein so far as sentiment, which is
never wanting in this artist's pictures, is concerned.

The Post.

BOSTON, May 15th, 1882.

It goes without saying, then, that the latest work from his brush, now on exhibition at the gallery of John A. Lowell & Co., is his best. It is entitled LE REFUGIÉ. At an archway door, deep set in a stone casement, stands the figure of a young Huguenot gentleman, knocking for shelter from the enemies from whom he has just escaped. The graceful pose of the figure and the expression of anxious suspense in the listening attitude, the startled look in the eyes and even in the tense lines of the face are in the strongest degree dramatic and intensely pathetic. The strength of the picture lies in its deep human interest and in the sympathy that it calls forth from the beholder, who almost instinctively longs to see the door open and the hunted refugee step within safe from harm. This element in the picture lies beyond all mere technical excellence, and the power to call out this feeling stamps it as a great work of art. In color and in handling it is remarkably fine. It is painted in low, harmonious tones, accented here and there with a bit of bright color, so that the whole effect is very rich. In felicity and delicacy of treatment, it suggests Meissonier.

The Advertiser.

BOSTON, May 18, 1882.

I. M. Gaugengigl is just giving the finishing touches to the largest painting he has ever made, and in almost all respects the most important of his works. It has been on his easel for several months past, and a great deal of time and labor have been spent upon it. The dimensions are not large, except in comparison with his former works, but the composition is elaborate and original to a degree seldom observed. On the seashore a duel has just been fought in the early morning. The landscape is beautifully painted,— a stretch of the sandy beach, at the right the smooth expanse of water, over which a faint morning haze hangs, and at the left a bit of rising ground, a sort of dune covered with short grass, on the crest of which an old-fashioned carriage (which has borne the combatants to the field and is to carry all save one away) is visible. The centre of the foreground is occupied by a dramatic group composed of four figures. The unfortunate duellist lies on his back, his head toward us, and his right arm extended at full length with his sword in the now powerless hand.

The two seconds are bending over him, in attitudes which unmistakably express their tardy
horror and sudden pity. One of them kneels,
and, with his head lowered close to the body of
the fallen man, places one hand over his heart
to ascertain if it beats yet. The victor is standing a little apart, at the right, and is sheathing
his blade with a theatrical gesture of bravado,
as much as to say, "He brought it upon himself." This haughty personage bears a decided
resemblance to the artist. All of the characters
in this serious drama are attired in the rich old
Spanish costumes for which Mr. Gaugengigl
has such an unconquerable predeliction. The
dying man is clothed in pink, and a hat of the
same color, which has rolled off from his head,
lies on the ground. The other men are equally
gay in attire, and have evidently been spending
the night at a ball or a banquet, where the
quarrel, now fatally concluded, had its origin
and culmination, whether it proceeded from a
game of cards, a family feud of long standing,
or a love affair — but this is immaterial. The
picture tells its story, as Mr. Gaugengigl's
pictures always do, with dramatic force and
directness. The grouping is capital, and each
figure is finely characterized. The landscape

is, as has been stated, beautifully painted. It is a genuine out-door effect, fresh and vigorous in quality, the sky soft and full of the delicate play of morning lights. The contrast between the soft beauty of the scene and the ugly human tragedy intruding into its calm midst, cannot fail to lend a peculiar interest to this original and striking work.

The Folio.

BOSTON, June, 1882.

J. M. Gaugengigl, the painter of those bits of character study that John A. Lowell & Co. have taken hold of lately, has just finished another one, representing a French refugee of the '98 days, his rich dress dusty but still neat in spite of it all, knocking at a door, behind which he is ignorant as to whether are awaiting friends or foes. There is a weariness over the strength of the face, and a shade of sadness and doubt, that are expressed in a tender and a touching way. The details of the picture are painted with great nicety and conscientiousness, the color is delicate and in some phases delicious, and as a whole it is a fine bit of pathetic sentiment.

The Journal.

Boston, June 3, 1883.

Mr. Gaugengigl is exhibiting at the rooms of Mr. John A. Lowell his latest picture. As Affair of Honor, describing a duel between men in the costume of a former century upon the shore of the sea. The work is the largest that this artist has produced here, with the exception of course of the few interior decorations from his brush, and differs from most of his other paintings in giving quite as much importance to landscape as to figures. The scene of action is upon a smooth and sandy beach under a hill, upon the top of which, strongly projected against the sky, appears a coach with four horses attached, and the driver on the box interestedly viewing the incident. The fight is just ended; one of the combatants, erect and unharmed, is sheathing his sword, and the other lies prostrate, still holding his weapon in his outstretched and stiffening hand. Over the latter bend the two seconds, one of them with his ear pressed against the breast of the wounded man in an attempt to hear the beating of his heart, but which, it is evident, is forever silenced. There is great variety and expression

in the attitudes of the men, and the foreshortening of the prostrate figure and that with its back
to the spectator is admirably done. The pose
of the victorious swordsman is imperious and
haughty — a trifle theatrical perhaps, yet even
in this respect not out of keeping with the man's
general appearance. A likeness of the artist
himself may be detected in this figure. The
coloring of the group is brilliant but harmonious, and finely related to the general chromatic
scheme of the work. Not the least success is
that which has been gained in the relation to
each other of the parts of the picture — the sky,
full of light clouds, the duller colored sea, the
main group of actors, the hill and the coach
upon it. Considering the difficulties of the task
proposed, and the successful way in which they
have been surmounted, this must be considered
to be one of Mr. Gaugengigl's very best works,
as it is also one of the most interesting.
Although the general public has not heretofore
been much acquainted with his work in landscape, those who have had a personal knowledge
of the wide range of his study of art, are not
surprised, although they cannot but be pleased,
with his present work in this direction. A
work of pure landscape from his brush is some-

thing we hope one day to have an opportunity
to inspect.

***

The Herald.

BOSTON, June 3. 1882.

Gaugengigl's latest painting is quite different
from the usual character of his work in that the
background to the little figures is a landscape
instead of being architectural, or combining
the accessories of an interior. This picture
describes the scene of a duel with the old-time
costuming, particularly appropriate to this old-
time custom. The figures of the participants
are diminutive — almost too small, in fact, to
create much interest. But they are well grouped
and drawn, and they are effectively contrasted
in color with the really fine gray tone of the
landscape, which is warm and lighted by a
luminous, pearly sky. The central group of
figures is balanced by a coach and horse in
waiting on a hill-slope in the middle distance.
This is a clever and creditable work, but one
would be willing to accept less technical excellence from this painter, now and then, if he
would only give some indication of the sentiment required to leaven the artistic loaf. It

may be ungracious to express this desire, for
Mr. Gaugengigl has given us some charming
little pictures, which are quite unique among
our art productions. But it should be remem-
bered that a good thing stimulates the taste and
excites a demand for more; whereas, from the
giver of a poor thing we neither ask nor wish
for more.

The Post.

BOSTON, June 3, 1882.

The largest, most ambitious, and in many respects the most important picture that Mr. I. M.
Gaugengigl has ever painted is the one which
he has recently completed and which is now
in the gallery of John A. Lowell & Co. It is
called the AFFAIR OF HONOR and represents a
duel scene. The picture is a bold composition,
and strikes the mind at once with its strong
dramatic force. The attitude and air of the
victor in the duel is very remarkable. There is
a scornful, pitiless look upon his face, and an
expression that no one can mistake, as if he
were haughtily throwing the blame for the affair
upon the dead man before him. The accessories
heighten the impressive effect of the group in
the foreground, and are not less well painted

than the figures. Especially is this true of the desolate beach and the sea and a bit of sky to the left, which are so studied in harmony with the rest of the work that they measurably add to its feeling of solemnity, its tragical mood.

The Times.

BOSTON, June 4, 1882.

Mr. I. M. Gaugengigl has finished his painting entitled, L'AFFAIRE D'HONNEUR, and it is now hung in the gallery of Messrs. John A. Lowell & Co., on exhibition. It is a large canvas, and represents three male figures in the foreground, clad in the French costume of the last century: one figure lies on the ground, another leans over him, while the third bends with eagerness to hear the first word of opinion concerning the wounded man. Some distance away stands the dignified figure of a man, who is putting his sword into its sheath, and he seems to say, "I have now had satisfaction." On the brow of the rising ground, to the left, outlined against the sky, is a stage coach of the time, with driver and horses in waiting. This little object is an essential part of the scene. It tells of the determined intention of the party to get away from the eyes of the curious, and that a long journey had been made. From the middle distance to the perspective the sea catches the glow of sunlight, the clouds being light, with a blue sky occasionally showing. In the group of figures there is some good foreshortening, better than is usually exhibited in this country while the drawing is throughout after Mr. Gaugengigl's usual careful style. In the selection and placing of the colors of the costumes, a rich harmony in variety occurs. The spot all about is desolate, and one that would be selected for some such deed. The composition is bold and impressive, and though there are objects larger and more conspicuous than the figures, still the duel scene holds the mind. Refined and delicate in all parts, the picture may be said to be Mr. Gaugengigl's finest achievement thus far.

The Globe.

BOSTON, June 4, 1882.

*   *   *   *   *

A picture, the exhibition of which at any time would be an event, can now be seen at Lowell's gallery — Mr. Gaugengigl's AN AFFAIR OF HONOR —which he has just completed. It repre-

sents the closing scene of a duel which has just
taken place on a sandy stretch of beach, with a
grass-covered hill slowly rising in the background. At its top, in the distance stands an
old-fashioned coach, waiting to carry away the
party. At the right is a narrow strip of sea,
smooth and silvery.   The sky is flushing with
the morning light, the sun evidently just rising
at the right behind the hill, and the light re-
flected from the sea glowing faintly in the sky
on the other side.   In the foreground the victor
is sheathing his sword, with head thrown back,
countenance and figure expressive of contempt
for the poor wretch with the death pallor on his
face who lies stretched at full length upon the
sand.   Over him bend the two seconds, one
with his back to the viewer, the other with con-
cern on his countenance, his flushed face con-
trasting with the pale one below.   The party
have evidently, from their gay attire, rushed
from some place of merry-making in the early
morning light to settle their difference in this
lonely place. Mr. Gaugengigl has succeeded
well in the painting of the landscape, an unusual subject with him.   The effects of the early
morning light, the clear, still, pure atmosphere,
are especially noteworthy.   Mr. Gaugengigl's

power of putting expression into the attitudes as well as the countenances of his figures is well known, but he has never succeeded better in this particular than in the present picture. The figure of the victorious duellist might well stand for the personation of malignant contempt.

The Globe.

BOSTON, June 25, 1882.

At Lowell's gallery Mr. Gaugengigl's new picture, ADAGIO, was put on exhibition last Friday. It represents a monk clad in a pale brown robe, from which protrudes one bare foot, playing on a violoncello. It tells an entirely different story of monkish life from the roystering scenes which many artists love to portray. The expression of the face is that of quiet interest in the music. but back of this absorption it tells also the story of long seclusion, of much thought, of severe struggles with temptations,—in short, it tells the whole story of the serious life of a conscientious monk. The technical execution, as in all of Mr. Gaugengigl's work, is very fine. The chief interest of the picture centres in the facial expression of the single figure, and it is in the portrayal of this that Mr. Gaugengigl's greatest excellence mainly lies.

BOSTON, July 1, 1882.

Messrs. John A. Lowell & Co. have just placed on exhibition Mr. Gaugengigl's last picture, the ADAGIO. The composition is simple and artistic in a marked degree. It is an interior,—the old monk absorbed in his 'cello, which rests before him, his fingers straying over the strings, the whole countenance expressive of its one purpose in musical art. There is an atmosphere, a sentiment to this picture that well repays study, and it is a beauty that impresses itself peculiarly on the visitor.

The Journal.

BOSTON, July 1, 1882.

Mr. I. M. Gaugengigl, who sails for Europe in a few days and will spend the summer abroad, has finished work for the season by painting a small picture entitled, ADAGIO, which is now on exhibition at the rooms of Messrs. John A. Lowell & Co., No. 70 Kilby Street. The painting represents a young monk, seated in his cloister cell and playing upon a violoncello. His music is held before him by a large book, which rests upon a wooden stool of antique pattern, and

the player wholly absorbed in the business that
engages him. The expression of a slow and
measured movement is well presented throughout, not only in the attitude of the bow and the
hand which controls the strings, but also in the
quiet, almost mournful expression of the per-
former, whose whole habit is evidently that of a
man inured to privation and devoted to his life
of seclusion and abstention from the uses of the
world, while he also possesses a poetic mind and
thoughts which gain an inspiration beyond the
bare walls of the convent. In completeness and
symmetry of intellectual idea, this is one of
the most successful of Mr. Gaugengigl's works.
The best piece of work in the picture is the bare
foot of the monk, which rests upon the floor,
half-escaped from the gray folds of the robe.
Nothing could be better than its solidity and
truth of drawing — and a foot foreshortened as
this is, is not an easy thing to describe — and its
coloring is simply wonderful in its tone and gra-
dations. It also pitches the key for the reds
which appear so prominently in the work, addi-
tional strength being gained for this color in the
lighted portions of the instrument, and its greatest intensity reached in the scarlet edges of the
leaves of the book upon the chair.

St. Louis Times-Democrat.

Sept. 1, 1882.

Mr. Lowell has literally made a future for the artist Gaugengigl, a young and gifted painter, who had, as is common among artists, far more genius than commercial ability. Mr. Lowell has the latter and the most discriminating appreciation of the former. Indeed he is an artist himself, only that he devotes his time more largely to business. and he introduced the pictures of the young Gaugengigl to the public. They are now selling from $500 up, and within two years will bring four times that amount.

The Times.

NEW YORK, Nov. 4, 1882.

*   *   *   *   *   *   *

I. M. Gaugengigl, in his L'AFFAIRE D'HON-NEUR, THE SURPRISE, ADAGIO, and LE REF-UGIÉ, substantiates the good judgment of Mr. Lowell in making an arrangement which secures to the latter all of his work.

The News.

LONDON, Nov. 25, 1882.

* * * * * * *

Gaugengigl, a Bavarian by birth, but a naturalized Bostonian, is already called the "American
Meissonier": he paints small *genre* in the manner of the famous French artist, and his work is
so far in demand that one has been stolen from
a public gallery, and, in spite of a large reward,
is still unrecovered; and Mr. Lowell has just
sold a tiny AFFAIRE D'HONNEUR for a thousand
dollars.

The Daily Advertiser.

BOSTON. Nov. 27, 1882.

I. M. Gaugengigl has finished a picture called
THE AMATEUR, which he began to paint in Germany during the summer. It is now on view in
the gallery of John A. Lowell & Co., 70 Kilby
Street, who last week sold his ADAGIO to a
Rhode Island gentleman for $500. This seems
a high price for a painting not much larger than
the palm of a man's hand, and so it would be, if
the value of works of art could be measured by
their size; but in fact it is perfectly natural and
inevitable that the market value of such pictures

as Mr. Gaugengigl's should increase in propor-
tion to the increase of taste, wealth and knowledge, and we should not be surprised to see his
four-by-six paintings sold for thousands a few
years hence where they are sold for hundreds
now. THE AMATEUR is like his former productions, with a few exceptions,—a single figure, as
diminutive as the husband of Mother Goose
memory, "no bigger than my thumb." He is
a vocalist, and seems to be rehearsing some
thorny passage in a song. It is probably the
point at which he takes his high C, for he has
opened his mouth to its greatest extent, and
steps forward on his right foot, lifting his right
hand high in the air with a gesture of genuine
operatic *abandon.* He is attired in a gaudy scarlet coat, a striped purple and yellow waistcoat,
and silk breeches, and hose of that creamy tint
that Mr. Gaugengigl knows so well how to paint.
He stands on a bearskin rug, and a purple cur-
tain is visible at his left. His hair is dishevelled,
and the contortions of his features reveal graphically the strenuous effort with which his whole
being is torn, as it were. This is one of Mr.
Gaugengigl's most humorous conceptions, and
in its execution he has left little or nothing to
be desired.

The Journal.

BOSTON, Dec. 2, 1882.

Mr. Gaugengigl has placed in the gallery of John A. Lowell & Co., his latest painting, which he calls THE AMATEUR. It is of a single figure, as most of this artist's works are, but rather larger than is usual with him, and describes a young male person, who, either struck with a mania for the honors of the stage, or cast for some part in private theatricals, is practising his lines with an earnestness and a profusion of gesture which should insure him an instantaneous and unequivocal success before any intelligent audience. He has evidently reached the climax of an exciting situation; his right hand is raised to its fullest extent: the whole body stretches out to follow it; the youth rises on tip-toe to give the impressiveness of increased attitude to the discharge of his burning periods; his hair is flying about and his gorgeous striped waistcoat is disarranged; his mouth is wide open evidently about to belch forth invective, and he looks into the book which he holds in his left hand to make sure he has got all the words right for the outburst. The absorbing interest of the man in his work,

his full satisfaction that he will make a sensation
when the time comes, and the conviction with
which he impresses the spectator, that he is a
smug, self-opinionated, good-humored noodle,
makes the picture one of the most amusing and
human that Mr. Gaugengigl has painted. The
technical work is, as usual, exquisite, particularly
fine being the careful and free painting of the
face, and the description of the texture and
wrinkles of the satin breeches.

The Tribune.

NEW YORK, Dec. 4, 1882.

* * * * * *

The works of Mr. Gaugengigl, a very clever
painter of delicate cabinet and *genre* pictures,
have of late appreciated so rapidly in value
under the enterprising methods of this firm, that
one of them was recently sold for $1,000, which
is at least three times as much as would have
been asked for it a year ago. As this is a new
venture, Mr. Lowell is naturally proceeding
cautiously, and is not taking up artists whose
works he is not reasonably sure of disposing of.
He now controls, as stated above, Mr. Gaugengigl's pictures, and also those of Mr. Waterman,
a fine painter of oriental subjects, Mr. Bick-

nell's black-and-whites and the works of a few
others.

The Journal.

BOSTON, Dec. 9, 1882.

Mr. I. M. Gaugengigl, who recently returned
from abroad, is busily engaged in developing
some ideas which he gained in Europe, as well
as advancing several pictures which he began
before leaving home. The work upon which he
is at the present moment actively employed
represents a young woman out driving, who is
holding some reins to which a spirited horse is
evidently attached, and is flying along at a high
rate of speed. The artist has succeeded admirably in expressing the idea of movement, which
he has heightened by introducing as a background a sky full of light clouds, which are
evidently blown by the wind in an opposite
direction. The picture is as yet hardly more
than a sketch, but its motive is as evident as if it
were completely finished. Mr. Gaugengigl, indeed is always skillful in expressing at the outset
of his work the purpose that is to direct him to
its close, and his sketches are as interesting as
his finished paintings, as far as suggestiveness
is concerned. Take for instance, another sketch

this energetic person. The other man, however,
who wears a blue coat, grey-green satin breeches.
white silk stockings and pointed shoes, is evidently a most unconscionable sceptic. He lolls
in his chair in an attitude which is not altogether polite or deferential, has his hands clasped
behind his head, wears his cocked hat upon the
knee of his left leg, which is crossed at it's ankle
above the other, and aggravatingly pats the
ground with his right foot. His expression of
countenance is most offensive to an earnest arguer. It is composed of equal parts of composure,
determination not to be convinced, and supercilious surprise that his friend should be such an ass
as to try to stuff *him* with any such nonsensical
rubbish. The humorous expression of the work
is most engaging, and grows on one by study.
The drawing and painting of the group are
masterly, and the row of chairs along the wall
is described with an unusual skill in solving a
difficult problem in perspective.

The Gazette.

BOSTON, Feb. 18, 1883.

A new picture by Gaugengigl is on exhibition
at Lowell's gallery called INCREDULITY, repre-

that he has recently made, in which two men in
French costume of the last century sit together
on a bench in a garden before a closely-cropped
hedge. The man in the light red coat, and with
a huge cocked hat on his head, is engaged in
high argument with his companion, who wears
a blue coat and balances his own monstrous hat
upon the knee of his left leg, which is thrown
over and rests its ankle on the right. The man
with the red coat has his back toward the foreground, but every line of his figure shows that
he is terribly in earnest. The man in the blue
coat, however, has made up his mind; his right
foot pats the ground coolly and tantalizingly, his
arms are folded behind his head, and he is evidently not to be moved. The argumentative
mood of the one and the pig-headed obstinacy
of the other are unmistakable, although the
sketch is a mere outline filled with flat color, and
only the faintest suggestion of features appear.
A third picture for which studies have been
made will represent the interior of an anteroom
in a richly appointed library. In the centre sits
an individual who has been reading aloud from
a book for the edification of a companion, who
lounges on a chair in the corner. The reader
has evidently heard a snore, and, looking

angrily around, as under the circumstances is quite natural, he perceives that his audience is calmly slumbering. There is here a fine opportunity for the expression of quiet humor and knowledge of human nature which the artist, with his well-known skill in such work, may be depended upon to improve.

The Magazine of Art.

February, 1883.

In America considerable attention has been attracted of late by the works of two clever young painters: I. M. Gaugengigl and George W. Edwards. The first, a Bavarian by birth, but a naturalized resident of Boston, U. S. A., has already won for himself the title of the "American Meissonier," and a tiny work of his, L'AFFAIRE D'HONNEUR, in the French master's manner, has just been sold for a thousand dollars. His works are in so great demand that one has already been stolen from the walls of an exhibition, and a large reward been offered for information as to its whereabouts. He studied at Munich, and also in Italy and France, and works slowly.

BOSTON, February, 1883.

Mr. I. M. Gaugengigl has just completed and placed on exhibition a new picture entitled INCREDULITY. It represents two men clad in costumes of the time of the Directory, sitting in cane-bottomed chairs before a plastered wall in a garden. The figure nearer the foreground, who has on a black cocked hat, a red coat, buff colored leather breeches and boots with yellow tops and cords, has his back turned toward the spectator, and only the side of his face can be seen. It is not necessary, however, to see his features, for every line in his expressive and admirably posed figure is full of animation, and the evident earnestness of his discourse is enough to carry conviction of the force of his argument to every candid mind. Moreover, he has in his left hand a paper which clearly substantiates the truth of what he is saying. He holds this in a grasp that is full of confidence, and taps it with the fingers of his right hand in a way that shews his own unwavering faith in the support which it gives to his position. No man was ever more fully assured of the truth of a thing or more anxious to convert another to his opinion than this energetic person. The other man, however, who wears a blue coat, grey-green satin breeches, white silk stockings and pointed shoes, is evidently a most unconscionable sceptic. He lolls in his chair in an attitude which is not altogether polite or deferential, has his hands clasped behind his head, wears his cocked hat upon the knee of his left leg, which is crossed at it's ankle above the other, and aggravatingly pats the ground with his right foot. His expression of countenance is most offensive to an earnest arguer. It is composed of equal parts of composure, determination not to be convinced, and supercilious surprise that his friend should be such an ass as to try to stuff *him* with any such nonsensical rubbish. The humorous expression of the work is most engaging, and grows on one by study. The drawing and painting of the group are masterly, and the row of chairs along the wall is described with an unusual skill in solving a difficult problem in perspective.

The Gazette.

BOSTON, Feb. 18, 1883.

A new picture by Gaugengigl is on exhibition at Lowell's gallery called INCREDULITY, repre-

senting two gentlemen of the old school seated
in a garden in rush-bottom chairs near a plastered wall. The figures are capitally drawn,
and tell the story in an admirable manner.

The Daily Advertiser.

BOSTON, Feb. 20, 1883.

The latest work from the brush of I. M. Gaugengigl is now on exhibition in the gallery of
John A. Lowell & Co. It is called INCREDULITY.
Two French gentlemen of the period of the
Directory are delineated at a moment when engaged in earnest argument, that is to say, one of
them is arguing while the other impatiently
listens with an air of unconquerable dissent and
scepticism. They are sitting in a garden, in the
shade of a high stuccoed wall, against which is
arrayed a long row of cane-bottomed chairs, and
over which clamber some leafy vines. Flowers
are blooming on the side of the gravel walk in
the foreground. A small section of blue sky is
visible above the wall. The power of expression.
which has always been Mr. Gaugengigl's most
prominent gift. is perhaps as finely exemplified
in this picture as in any that has come from his
easel. His ability as a story-teller has never

been greater. The serious emphasis with which
his figure seems to be talking (though his face
is not seen at all) is unmistakable. All this is
expressed in his attitude, the lines of his back
and head, the movement of his arm and hand.
The stubborn state of mind of the listener and
passive opponent is quite as well set forth, both
by his attitude of impatience and the immovable
obstinacy of character revealed by his countenance, which says as plainly as words could say :
" You see I will hear you through with the utmost
courtesy, but I do not believe a word of it, I
disagree with you utterly, and when I can get a
word in edgewise I will promptly demolish your
whole argument." The costumes of these two
characters are particularly sumptuous, even for
Mr. Gaugengigl, who, we suspect, has a sort of
barbaric penchant for a tremendous blaze of rich
colors, which do not always escape some discord
among themselves. The modelling of the
figures and the painting of the satin breeches of
one of the men are wholly admirable.

The Sunday Herald.

BOSTON, Feb. 25, 1883.
In the group of Gaugengigl's paintings, at the

Lowell Art Gallery, may be seen a combination
of qualities quite distinctive from those of American productions, and it might, perhaps, be said,
from the tastes or possibilities of our own truly
national artists. The little figures that Mr. Gaugengigl uniformly paints bear the marks of foreign costumes and manners, and are placed in
surroundings the picturesqueness and harmony of
which can only be suggested by foreign scenes.
Much of the interest of these pictures arises undoubtedly from the very familiarity of the facts
presented and because they are the only exam-
ples of their kind to be seen here. But a stronger
feature of their attractiveness is the skillful technique of the works, refined blending of color,
and the generally pleasing motives of the work.
There is a slight vein of humor often expressed
by these little pictures, so that they only arouse
agreeable feelings, and may always be counted
upon to win a smile. So light is their sentiment
or humor that the expression cannot become
tiresome. Accordingly, the paintings are especially adapted to the drawing-room easel,
where they are at home amid elegant surroundings, and where they will continually exert an
influence of refined mirth. The latest addition
to this group of four or five paintings is called

INCREDULITY. The scene depicted presents the figure of a man sitting against a stuccoed wall along which are ranged a row of chairs, running off into the distance, suggesting a pleasure garden by their presence and the growth of flowers bordering the gravel walks. By the side of the man, whose face is fully presented to us, another is seen whose back only is in view. He is telling, evidently, a preposterous story into the ear of his unbelieving neighbor. The figures are full of life and comical in their graphic expressiveness. The color and composition are, as usual, very clever and interesting, and the costumes belong to the era of quaintness and color. But of all the collection, the others of which have been previously described, the figure of the red-bonneted little woman with a leopard skin over her lap and her arms extended in the act of driving, is the most thoroughly charming. It is full of piquant spirit, and in color is as brilliant and full as a ruby. The pictures collectively are even more than individually interesting.

PROVIDENCE, March 2, 1883.

*   *   *   *   *   *   *

Most unique among the pictures are four by
I. M. Gaugengigl, which, for masterly draughts-
manship, fine coloring, and interest of subject
can hardly be excelled. BELLISSIMA, the girl
driving, is one of which *The Press* has before
spoken. INCREDULITY is his last picture — two
gentlemen of the Directoire period sitting in a
public garden; the older one evidently telling
some tale of Baron Munchausen hugeness to his
very incredulous listener, who, bored to death,
leans against his hands and listens. THE SUR-
PRISE has a flavor of gallantry and fun about it
that is irresistible when we notice that the surprised maiden, while she screams at the top of
her lungs, evidently enjoys the situation and
falls very gracefully into the arms of her lover.
THE REFUGEE represents a young Huguenot
chevalier who has escaped from the officers of
the cruel Queen Catharine De Medici, and is
knocking at the door of a friend's house, half
hoping, half fearing. Mr. Lowell has engaged
all the work of Mr. Gaugengigl.

Saturday Evening Gazette.

[Speaking of the Loan Collection at the Museum of Fine Arts.]

Nov. 3, 1883.

Among the *genre* pictures, Mr. Gaugengigl's A QUIET AFTERNOON (No. 112) bears the palm. It is a delightful little work, quiet in tone and full of charm both in color and treatment. The drawing is very careful, and the finish throughout is perfect, but it has been achieved without loss of breadth or grace.

To the Reader.

INFORMATION concerning the paintings of I. M. GAUGENGIGL can be obtained at any time by application to JOHN A. LOWELL & COMPANY, No. 70 Kilby Street, Boston, Mass., U. S. A., who have the exclusive control of all this artists' works.